1

AND THESE ARE THEIR ADVENTURES!

SWEET DREAMS, SEWER RATS!

Scholastic Inc.

www.geronimostilton.com

Published by Scholastic Inc., *Publishers since 1920*, 557 Broadway, New York, NY 10012. SCHOLASTIC and associated logos are trademarks and/or registered trademarks of Scholastic Inc.

ISBN 978-1-338-18272-9

Text by Geronimo Stilton
Original title *La lunga notte dei supertopi*
Original design of the Heromice world by Giuseppe Facciotto and Flavio Ferron
Cover by Giuseppe Facciotto (design) and Daniele Verzini (color)
Illustrations by Luca Usai (pencils), Valeria Cairoli (inks), and Serena Gianoli and Daniele Verzini (color)
Graphics by Francesca Sirianni and Chiara Cebraro

Special thanks to Joanne Ruelos Diaz
Translated by Anna Pizzelli
Interior design by Kevin Callahan/BNGO Books

10 9 8 7 6 5 4 3 2 1 17 18 19 20 21

Printed in the U.S.A. 40

First printing 2017

When darkness falls over Muskrat City, the Sewer Rats slither into the alleys to cause chaos aboveground. But the citizens of Muskrat City know that there are mysterious figures watching over them, ready to fight evil at all costs.

They are strong, they are invincible, they are fearless — well, almost . . .

They are the Heromice!

Nothing is impossible for the Heromice!

MEET THE HEROMICE!
GERONIMO SUPERSTILTON
The strongest hero in Muskrat City . . . but he still must learn how to control his powers!
SWIFTPAWS
Geronimo Superstilton's partner in crimefighting; he can transform his supersuit into anything.
LADY WONDERWHISKERS
A mysterious mouse with special powers; she always seems to be in the right place at the right time.
TESS TECHNOPAWS
A cook and scientist who assists the Heromice with every mission.
ELECTRON AND PROTON
Supersmart mouselets who help the Heromice; they create and operate sophisticated technological gadgets.

The undisputed leader of the Sewer Rats; known for being tough and mean.

Sludge's right-hand mouse; the true (and only) brains behind the Sewer Rats.

Tony's wife; makes the important decisions for their family.

Bodyguards who act as Sludge's henchmice; they are big, buff, and brainless.

Tony and Teresa's teenage daughter; has a real weakness for rat metal music.

Good-bye, Blue-Cheese Bath!

Ahhh . . . there's nothing better than soaking in a **RELAXING BATH** with aromatic blue-cheese bath salts! I was just starting to melt into the **fragrant fizz** when—oops!

Pardon me! I haven't introduced myself! My name is *Stilton, Geronimo Stilton*, and I run *The Rodent's Gazette*, Mouse Island's most **famouse** newspaper.

Anyway, one evening I was on special assignment at New Mouse City's newest spa, **Furever Young**, researching the latest health and beauty treatments. It was hard work, but some mouse has to do it!

"Dear Stilton, come in, come in!" The manager, Monsieur le Rat, welcomed me warmly at the door as a waft of **STINKY CHEESE** tickled my snout. Ahhh! He handed me a brochure with a menu of indulgent options: a greasy-cheese total-fur conditioning, a ***soft-cheese hot towel whiskers treatment***, and a **full-body blue-cheese aromatherapy soak** in the hot tub. I couldn't wait!

In minutes, I was settling into the hot tub. The blue-cheese bath salts were beginning to bubble when . . .

Riiiing!

Moldy mozzarella! Who could be calling me?! I picked up the phone and heard a familiar voice.

"Geronimo! You're not *lounging* on your paws, are you?" my friend Swiftpaws bellowed. "I need you right away! Muskrat City needs the **STRENGTH** and bravery of the Heromice!"

"First of all, I'm not lounging on my paws. Second, I'm not strong or brave! I'm not cut out to be a Heromouse! And third, I'm taking a bubble bath, I mean, I'm working! I can't come . . ."

"Bath?! Bubbles can wait! You'd better run—actually fly—right away. I'll meet you at Swiss Square. There's no time to lose!" And with that, he hung up.

SQUEAK!

I leaped out of the hot tub, threw on my robe, and charged toward the changing room. Mousefully, there was no one around. I pulled the superpen that changes me into a Heromouse from my locker and opened the window. Brrr! Shivering, I transformed into Superstilton and flew off to Muskrat City.

It was so **dark** outside you couldn't tell a cat from a rat. But wait! What were those SPARKLING lights in the distance? I swooped down to **investigate**.

But of course! They were the lights of

MUSKRAT CITY.

I zoomed in for a closer look. It seemed like every streetlight, every skyscraper, and every BILLBOARD was shining brightly. I was so captivated by the show of lights that I didn't see the blimp flying right toward me!

Thwap!

The blimp hit me head on and sent me plunging down, down, down.

Fortunately, I quickly regained control of my supersuit and landed—**Snout first**—on the hard pavement.

"That landing was a bit of a *stinker*, eh, partner?" Swiftpaws chuckled.

"*Umph*," I mumbled. "I've had better!"

All-Night Party

As I stood up and massaged my aching snout, I did a DOUBLE TAKE. Swiss Square was busier than Mousemart on Black Friday. Swarms of mice surrounded a HUMONGOUS screen that was set up on a stage in the middle of the square.

TESS TECHNOPAWS, chef, scientist, and friend to the Heromice, scurried over, followed by the mouselets Electron and Proton.

"Good evening, Superstilton. Welcome to the Golden Sun Awards!" Tess said with a smile.

"The Golden Sun Awards?" I asked. "What in the name of cheese are those?"

Amazing!
Oh!
Wow!
Super Swiss slices!

Golden Sun Awards
Good evening!
Hello!

Electron giggled. "They're the sister awards to the famouse Golden Cheddar Film Festival," she explained patiently.

"That's right," Swiftpaws continued. "It's when Muskrat City honors the brightest stars in movies and television."

"It's one of the most unique and exciting events of the year. The party goes ALL NIGHT and ends when Mayor Pete Powerpaws gives out golden statues at SUNRISE!" Proton finished.

I looked around, and, for the first time, I noticed that the mice around me were dressed in their FANCIEST suits and gowns.

"Oh, well . . . thanks for the invitation,"

I replied. "But I thought there was an **emergency**. I was in the middle of a B A T H, I mean, er, important work. So if you'll excuse me—"

"Wait." Proton stopped me. "Swiftpaws hasn't told you yet?"

I took a deep breath. "No . . . not yet . . ."

Then I turned to my partner in crime-fighting. "Could you please tell me what's going on?"

"The police received a message from **Tony Sludge**!" Electron jumped in. "He said he has a plan for the Golden Sun Awards that will prove he's the ***Most Evil Crime Rat*** once and for all. The message said that Muskrat City will be **doomed** to suffer **DARK TIMES FOREVER**!"

"D-dark times?" I stammered. "F-f-forever?"

Proton nodded and went on. "We are on HIGH ALERT. It could mean anything. The mayor is desperate for the Heromice's help!"

"We're ready!" Swiftpaws declared. "We'll keep EYES and ears on every corner of Swiss Square. We'll chase every stray tail! No suspicious rat will get away!"

My partner's eyes DARTED past me. "Like that one!" he squeaked, pointing to a mouse with thick BROWN hair.

"That's Rob Squeak!" Electron exclaimed. "He plays the evil villain in the GALAXY SPACEMICE television series."

"Plays the evil villain, eh . . ." Swiftpaws mumbled. "We'll see about that! Come on, Superstilton! Hey? Superstilton?"

Before I could **SNEAK AWAY**, Swiftpaws had grabbed my cape and dragged me into the crowd.

Why, oh why, am I such a 'fraidy mouse?!

Fright Night

Before my *panic* completely set in, I heard a **cheerful** squeak.

"Superstilton! Swiftpaws! You're here, too!"

Priscilla Barr, Muskrat City's most famouse lawyer, stepped toward us wearing a ***shimmery blue*** dress that matched her **DAZZLING BLUE** eyes.

"Priscilla, we're on a mission!" Swiftpaws replied. "The Sewer Rats have a **secret plan** that threatens the awards ceremony—and all of Muskrat City!"

"The Sewer Rats?" she asked, stunned. "You must have your paws full!"

Overflowing is more like it! Just then, I felt a **sharp** pain on my tail.

"Ouch!" I cried.

Rob Squeak had spotted Priscilla from afar and pushed past me to get to her — stepping on my tail in the process! The star couldn't care less. He just swooped by and kissed Priscilla Barr on her paw.

"Delighted to meet you, Ms. Barr," he oozed. Then he tossed his snout in my direction.

"Was that poor little rat bothering you?" he asked, sneering.

I was too stunned (and in too much pain!) to defend myself.

"Please allow me," Rob Squeak drawled as

he gestured to the dance floor.

I'm pretty sure I saw Priscilla roll her eyes before she politely stepped into the party of dancers with him.

"**Crumbly Camembert!**"

Swiftpaws complained under his breath. "I wanted to **DANCE** with her!"

I was about to remind Swiftpaws of Sludge's evil plan when Electron and Proton came scrambling in our direction.

"I saw her!" Proton cried. "Here in the crowd!"

That got Swiftpaws's attention. "Who?!" he squeaked.

"ELENA SLUDGE! She's wearing dark sunglasses, but I can tell it's her. She's heading down that alley!"

Elena is Tony Sludge's doleful daughter. We scurried quickly after her, like a hungry rat chasing a wheel of cheese. But the alley was EMPTY.

Proton sighed. "I know I saw her. I'm PAWSITIVE!"

"And I'm PAWSITIVE you saw who you wanted to see," Electron quipped.

Proton blushed. He and Elena had

worked together in the past, and they were occasionally friends — but mostly enemies!

Swiftpaws strode back toward the **dance floor**. "We have to get back to Rob Squeak!" he said. "Who knows what he's up to?"

"Swiftpaws could be right," Proton said thoughtfully. "In *GALAXY SPACEMICE* season three, episode seven, Squeak's character, **Mork Mercury**, dressed up as a

Space Squad member when he was really working for the evil Asteroid Corp! So Rob Squeak really could be a SEWER RAT in disguise!"

We found the actor and trailed him from a tail's length away for what seemed like an eternity. But we didn't notice anything alarming, other than how much he seemed to love himself.

"There's no way he wants to ruin the ceremony," Electron noted. "He's so vain he would never miss his chance to accept the BEST LEADING MOUSE AWARD on live TV."

She had a point. And speaking of accepting awards . . . when would the CEREMONY start already?! My aching paws were killing me from standing for so long.

Swiftpaws must have felt the same way

How was it seven thirty in the morning?!

because he checked his watch. "**Super Swiss slices**, partner! It's seven thirty — in the **morning**!"

"Huh?" I asked, looking up at the night sky. "B-but it's s-still p-pitch d-dark out."

Just then, the mayor

stepped onto the stage. "Fellow citizens, we have a SITUATION. It's seven thirty in the morning, but it's still as DARK as *midnight*. Something is very wrong, but the HEROMICE are here to help us!"

Immediately, I felt a hot spotlight on my snout.

"Uh . . ." I muttered, shielding my eyes from the piercing light. "We, umm . . ."

"Wonderful!" Mayor Powerpaws said. "We know we can always count on the Heromice!"

YIKES! WHAT NOW?!

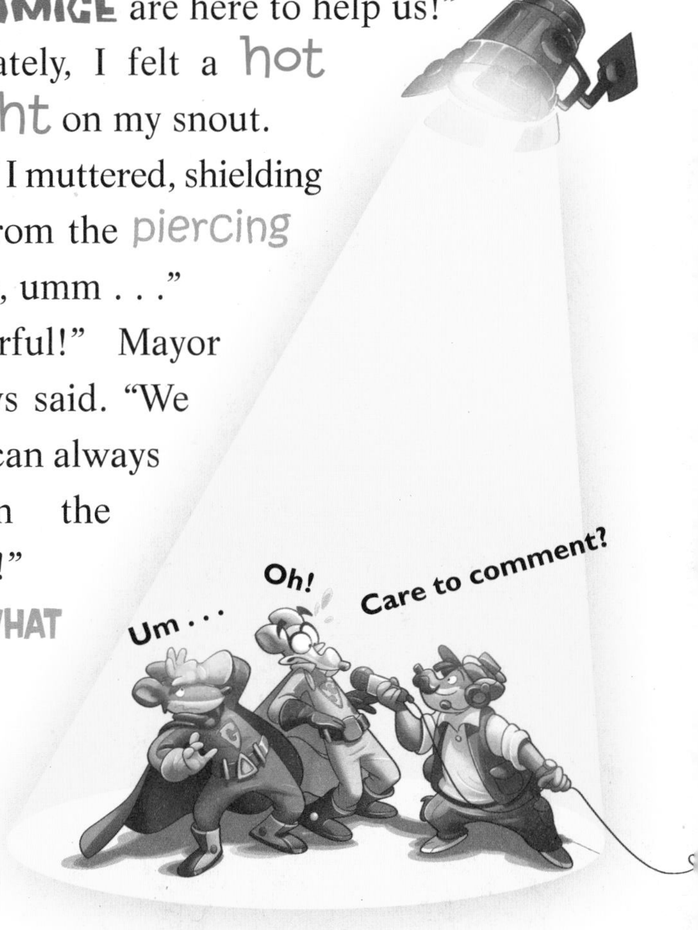

Dome of Doom

Panic spread through the crowd. Tess caught up with us, a worried look on her snout.

"Rancid ricotta, Heromice!" she exclaimed. "How can this be?! Muskrat City trapped in eternal darkness? Where's the **SUN**?! We have to get to the bottom of this."

"We're on it, Tess!" Swiftpaws declared. "**Supersuit: Rocket Mode!**"

He turned to me. "Ready, Superstilton?"

My tail began to **tremble**. "Well, uh . . . perhaps it would be better if I s-stayed h-here . . ."

Seeing my friends looking confused, I added, "How many times do I have to tell you?! I'm not cut out to be a Heromouse!"

"Ah, no worries, Superstilton," said Electron while Proton hooked some devices to my supersuit belt.

"Wait, w-wait," I stammered. "What are those things?"

"They're pocket-sized turbo-blasters!" explained Proton. "They'll help you blast off, then they'll turn off automatically."

"B-blast off?! What do you mean — Ahhh!"

Ahhh! Help!

Before I knew it, I was shooting straight up into the sky at superspeed with my partner beside me.

WHOOSH!

My stomach LURCHED as we zoomed higher into the NIGHT SKY. Then, suddenly, a blazing light blinded me. Great balls of mozzarella! Was this the end?! But no. It was sunlight. Up here, there was light! I looked down and realized we had flown through an ENORMOUSE BLACK DOME that was covering Muskrat City and completely blocking out the sun.

"Superstilton, we have to tell everyone!" Swiftpaws cried. "Superstilton? What are you doing?!"

Incredible!
How can this be?

What was I doing? I was plummeting. **Yikes!**

My pocket-sized **turbo-blasters** had malfunctioned. With **no control** over my supersuit, I was plunging toward the ground.

"Good thinking!" my superpartner said as he swooped down next to me. "We must hurry!"

Eek. I was hurrying alright! In fact, I was **CRASHING**!

Luckily, the roof of a Swiss Square food stall broke my fall. I **ROLLED** to the ground like a wheel of Parmesan. To my great surprise, **NOBODY** noticed. Every mouse was staring at the mega-screen, which was filled with the most **dangerous** and **terrifying** snout: **Tony Sludge**.

"Dear citizens of Muskrat City," he sneered with a sinister smile. "How do you like my little surprise? You pathetic rats will NEVER see the light of day again! Ha, ha, ha!

"I have created a **GIGANTIC DOME OF DOOM** that surrounds all of Muskrat City," the rat said gleefully. "Thanks to

Slickfur's latest invention, the Doomsday Desolarizer, no sunlight can reach your FAIR city."

The audience gasped.

"And that's not all," he continued. "At noon on the dot, the Dome of Doom will freeze and Muskrat City will be cold and DARK—FOREVER! Ha, ha, ha!"

With that, the screen went black.

Proton wasted no time and started tapping away on his laptop. "First we need to see if there are any electro-photo-atomic wave disturbances in the atmosphere . . ."

Whaaat?

MOLDY MUENSTER! What did that mean?!

Tess looked at me calmly and squeaked, "Don't worry, my dear. Proton is trying to figure out where Slickfur's invention

could be. If we find it, we can break it and destroy the dome."

Unfortunately, the mouselet had no luck.

"I can't **detect** any abnormalities in the atmosphere," Proton said with a sigh as Commissioner Rex Ratford approached.

"My POLICEMICE can sweep the city, but it will take a LONG time with no clues," the commissioner told us.

Just then I felt my **whiskers** tremble. I turned around and saw a **stunning** sight: It was Lady Wonderwhiskers, my favorite Heromouse!

Who Can You Trust?

Soon enough, Swiss Square was completely empty. The anxious crowds had scurried home in the dark.

"Lady Wonderwhiskers, you're here!" my superpartner squeaked.

"Of course!" she replied. "If Muskrat City is in DANGER, I'll always be here. Now, Tess, why is it so hard to find the location of the Doomsday Desolarizer?"

Tess took a deep breath. "PUTRID PEPPER JACK! The Sewer Rats did a good job hiding it. We can't find a signal, so it must be out of range."

"There has to be another way to find it!"

I said. "Right, Proton? Proton??"

But our young friend was pointing in front of him as if in a **trance**. "I told you it was her," he *whispered*.

"Huh, who?" asked Electron.

"Look!" I yelped, pointing with Proton. "*Someone's here!*"

Tony Sludge's daughter, **ELENA SLUDGE**, was standing in an alley by a streetlight. **Holey Havarti!** Proton had been right!

We hurried over to her.

"**ELENA SLUDGE**, what are you doing here?" Swiftpaws asked.

The mouselet sniffed. "None of your business!"

"I know!" Electron jumped in. "You must be here to monitor the **Doomsday Desolarizer**!"

"What?" Elena scoffed. "Don't be

ridiculous. I have nothing to do with Daddy's **anti-sun** whatever."

"Well, then . . ." Swiftpaws pressed. "Why are you here?"

Elena **BLUSHED** slightly, then looked at us defiantly. "I—I **ran away** from home. Happy now?!"

"You what?!" Electron squeaked. "You can't do that! You should know better!"

"I wanted to come to the **Golden Sun Awards**, but Daddy wouldn't let me, so I had to run away!" Elena lowered her eyes and added quietly, "But when he finds out, he'll ground me for life."

"And he'd be right for once . . ." Electron mumbled. She eyed Sludge's daughter. "Are you really telling us the **truth**?"

Elena rolled her eyes and opened her bag. "*GALAXY SPACEMICE* is my favorite show. I **adore** Rob Squeak. I had to have him *autograph* this for me!" She pulled out his headshot.

"Hey, what's that?" Proton asked, picking up a **piece of paper** that had fallen out of Elena's bag.

"What does it look like, smarty-pants?" Elena said sarcastically. "It's a headshot of—oh, that? It's just a ***MAP*** of Muskrat City from my dad's office. I used it to figure out how to get here."

I grabbed the **map** and pointed to

some **red X marks**. "Look!"

"If this **map** is from Tony's office," Tess began, "then those **red X marks** might indicate—"

"—where the **Doomsday Desolarizers** are located!" Swiftpaws, Lady Wonderwhiskers, and I squeaked in unison.

Heromice in Action!

Tess drew a line connecting the four red marks. "Ah, now it makes sense," she said. "There's not just one large device sending out one strong signal. I'll bet there are four smaller devices sending out weaker, undetectable ones. The machines might even be ELEVATED somehow to be closer to the sun."

I studied the map closely. "It looks like . . . there's one right where we are!" We looked up.

The blimp I had bumped earlier was directly overhead.

"That's it!" I squeaked. "It's the BLIMP!

The first Desolarizer must be inside!"

Lady Wonderwhiskers had made her own revelation. "It looks like a second one is at the Muskrat City TV studios!"

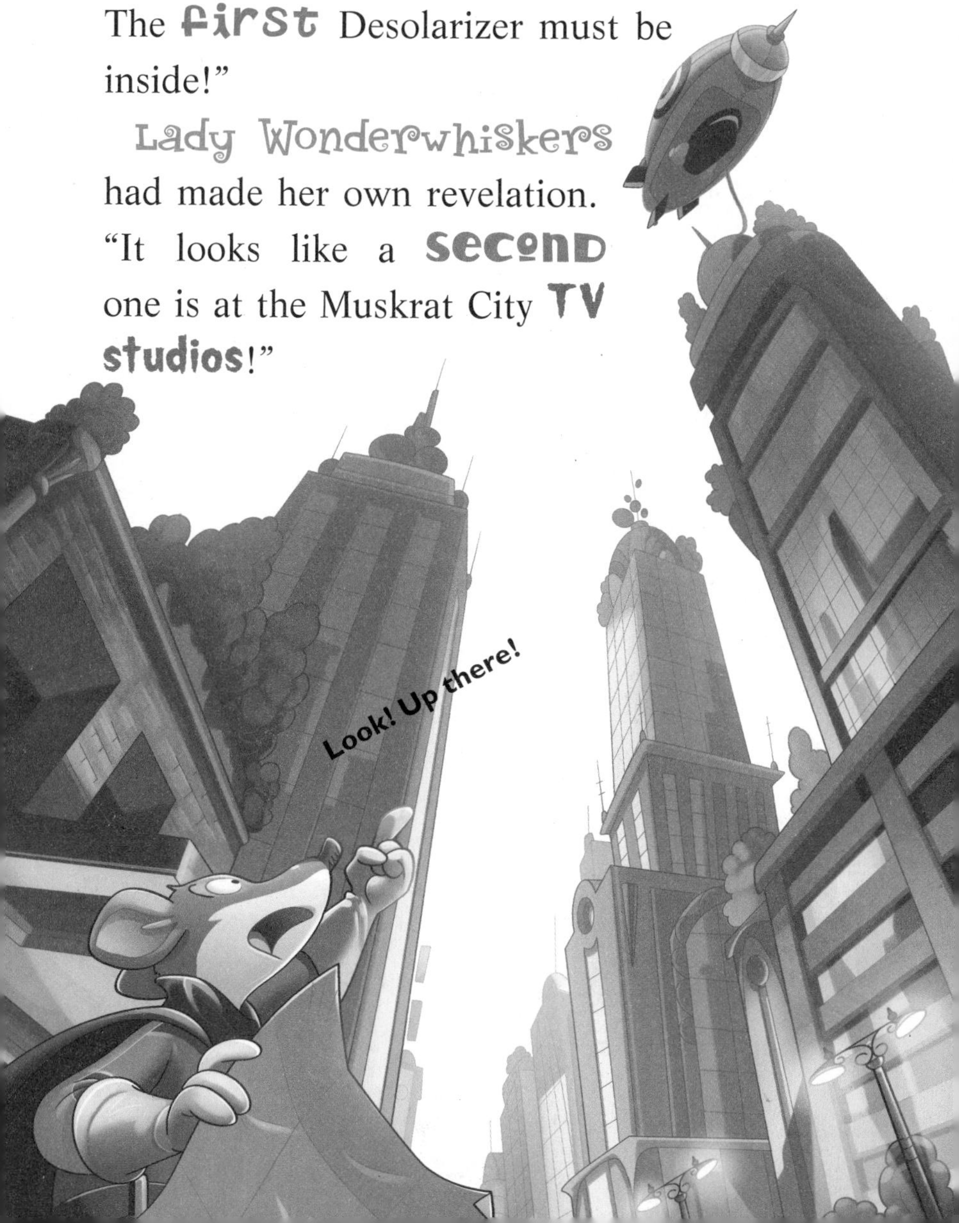

"But that's where **Rob Squeak's** show is filmed!" Elena said with a gasp.

"A **third** one might be at **Gouda Park**, Muskrat City's largest amousement park!" Proton interrupted, pointing to a third **X** on the map.

"And it looks like a **FOURTH** device is hidden in this warehouse area outside of town!" Electron concluded.

"**Peppered Pecorino!**" Swiftpaws exclaimed. "What are we waiting for? We have to deactivate them all!"

"It won't be easy," Commissioner Ratford warned. "Sludge probably has **henchmice** guarding each one."

"Not to mention that it's already nine a.m.," Tess added. "We have three hours until noon!"

"Then we'd better split up," Lady

Wonderwhiskers concluded.

"**PERFECT!**" Elena squeaked, grabbing Proton's paw. "We'll head to the ***TV STUDIO***."

Proton's whiskers started to **twitch**. "B-but, well, I, uh . . ."

"Elena, are you sure you want to help us?" I questioned her. "If your dad finds out, you'll be in even bigger **trouble**."

"That's right," Swiftpaws agreed. "And why do you want to help us, anyway?"

Elena hesitated for a moment. "Whatever," she said **hotly**. "I don't want to help you or Muskrat City. But Daddy has gone too far this time. How dare he try to ruin **Rob Squeak's** big night!"

Lady Wonderwhiskers decided to take matters into her own paws. "Okay, Elena! **Together** we will be even **stronger**. You can come with me!"

With that, Lady Wonderwhiskers, Elena, Proton, and Electron left for the TV studio and Swiftpaws and I headed for the **blimp**.

"**Heromice in action!** Supersuit: Superspeedy Superflying Scooter Mode!" Swiftpaws commanded.

I clutched my partner and closed my eyes as we shot into the air at top speed. *Eek! I'm not cut out to be a Heromouse!*

Yikes! Too fast!
Heromice to the rescue!
Good luck!

String-Cheese Bungee Jumping

We **whizzed** through the air above the dark, empty streets as we headed toward the **BLIMP**. I tried not to imagine another crash landing. **Why do I have to be afraid of heights?!**

As we approached the blimp, we saw a strong **steel** cable anchoring it to a tall building nearby. I **SQUINTED** and was able to see a faint **BLACK** beam shooting out from the blimp's cockpit.

"That's it, partner!" **Swiftpaws** cried. "We have to get inside the blimp!"

I wasn't so sure. "Um . . . remember what Commissioner Ratford said? There could

be **henchmice** in there! We'd better be care—"

SWOOOSH!

Something huge ***flew*** out of the blimp, stopping me midsentence. It was quickly followed by a second and a third object! They were none other than

Sludge's bodyguards, ONE, TWO, and THREE. And they were zooming straight at us on flying scooters!

"FLIPPING FONTINA!" Swiftpaws yelled. "We'd better split up, Superstilton!"

"Good idea, partner!" I shouted back. Then I took a deep breath and flew off on my own.

Right then, TWO turned and steered straight toward Swiftpaws.

"**Supersuit: Soccer-Ball Mode!**" my partner cried out.

Swiftpaws immediately transformed into a **black-and-white** ball and flew toward his **GOAL** — the Sewer Rat's belly!

Bonk!

"Well done, partner!" I cheered.

But there was no time to celebrate.

"Superstilton, watch out!" Swiftpaws warned.

ONE and **THREE** had caught up to me.

"***Grated Parmesan!***" I had been outmoused! Luckily, my superpowers activated and tons of grated cheese poured down on my pursuers, forcing them to pull back. Whew! **Saved by the cheese!**

But I couldn't sit back on my paws yet.

"Superstilton, behind you!" Swiftpaws hollered.

We've got you!
You're toast!
Oh nooo!
SUPERPOWER:
STORM OF GRATED PARMESAN
ACTIVATED WITH THE CRY:
"GRATED PARMESAN!"

It was too late. When I turned my snout, bam!

I hit the blimp—again!

I was plunging downward—again!

"Oh nooo!" I cried. "Superstringy mozzarella! I don't want to be kitty kibble!"

My superpowers sprang to action again. A rubbery string of mozzarella wrapped around my waist, and the other end stuck to the side of the blimp.

Boing! Thwap!

The string-cheese bungee rope tightened up and I rocketed into the air past the blimp. Boing! When the string cheese went slack,

Superstringy mozzarella!

SUPERPOWER:
MOZZARELLA
STRING-CHEESE
BUNGEE ROPE
ACTIVATED WITH
THE CRY:
"SUPERSTRINGY
MOZZARELLA!"

Help!

I dropped down again. Thwap!

"Help!" I cried. "I don't want to bungee-jump on a piece of string cheeeeeeeeeese!"

I swung back and forth until I was finally able to FLIP into the blimp's cockpit, where Swiftpaws was waiting for me.

"Nice dismount, partner!" he said with a grin.

"Oof . . . it's not funny," I mumbled, holding my *spinning* head.

"Let's turn this thing off," he replied, turning to the **Doomsday Desolarizer's** controls. "I'll just push some of these **buttons** . . ."

"Wait, **STOP**!" I cried, stepping toward him. "We don't know what these controls do. We should call Tess and—**Gah!**"

I had *TRIPPED* over a cable and unplugged it.

WHIRRR . . . CLICK.

Superstilton glanced at the machine and then looked out the blimp's window. "Great job, partner!"

"Huh?" I asked, then followed his gaze. **INCREDIBLE!** I couldn't believe my eyes.

The strange device had been turned off!

"That was as easy as cheese!" Swiftpaws squeaked, grinning. "We just needed to disconnect the power! Superstilton, you're a real Heromouse!"

SUPER E TO THE RESCUE!

Meanwhile, Lady Wonderwhiskers, Proton, Electron, and Elena were outside the **TV studio**.

"We have to get to the ROOF," Lady Wonderwhiskers whispered.

Proton sighed. "But how?"

"With these!" Electron replied. "They're one of Tess's latest inventions — supersuction climbing cups."

"Mouserific!" Proton squeaked.

They put on the new

gear and started **climbing**. Halfway up, Elena peeked through an open window and saw racks of COLORFUL JUMPSUITS, wild wigs, and funny hats.

"I have an IDEA," Elena squeaked. She snuck through the window and *disappeared*.

"What is she up to now?" Proton asked.

"Forget about it," Electron replied. "We shouldn't **trust** her. Let's go."

When they reached the building's roof, they spied **SLICKFUR**, Sludge's right-hand mouse, guarding the **Desolarizer**.

"Shhh!" Lady Wonderwhiskers murmured.

Proton went to **huddle** next to her, but he had forgotten to take off his **SUCTION CUPS**. He lost his balance and fell to the ground with a *thunk*!

"**WHO'S THERE?!**" Slickfur growled.

Lady Wonderwhiskers stepped forward boldly. "Turn **off** that machine right now!"

"**HA!** I don't think so," Slickfur retorted. Then he aimed a **STRANGE-LOOKING** device at her.

It looked like a big **FLASHLIGHT**, but instead of a beam of light, a **black ray** shot out and **struck** my favorite Heromouse!

"Aah!" she yelped. "I can't see!"

"How do you like my **BE BLIND BLASTER**?" The evil Sewer Rat smirked. "Get in its path and you won't be able to see a **paw** in front of your **snout**."

"Drop that blaster!" said a new voice.

"Or else what?" Slickfur demanded.

"You'll have to deal with me!"

The mice turned and saw a figure wearing a **purple supersuit** with a **letter E** patch

on the front and a glowing green cape.

Slickfur scoffed. "And who are **YOU**?"

"I am Super E, the newest and most powerful HEROMOUSE!"

"Oh yeah?" Slickfur interrupted. "Well, take this, Super E!"

He pointed the BE BLIND BLASTER at the mysterious stranger. She avoided its **BEAM** by jumping quickly to the side.

"WOW!" marveled Proton.

Meanwhile, the blaster's effect on Lady Wonderwhiskers had worn off. When Slickfur aimed at her again, she pulled out a small mirror and reflected the beam back at him.

"Aaargh!" the Sewer Rat cried, rubbing his eyes. He staggered toward the Desolarizer and knocked it over. It wobbled and fell with a loud crash.

Lady Wonderwhiskers smiled as Slickfur scurried away. "Great COSTUME, Elena!" she whispered.

The mouselet smiled proudly. "Daddy's henchmouse will never know it was me!"

"Let's update the team!" Lady Wonderwhiskers said. "The second Doomsday Desolarizer is out of commission!"

Blast this!
Aaargh!

Along Came a Spider . . .

"**HELLO?**" Swiftpaws answered the call on his Heromouse watch. "Oh, Lady Wonderwhiskers! Everything okay over there?"

Once we heard the successful news from the gang at the TV studio, we agreed to meet them at the amousement park to help Commissioner Ratford.

We all ***RUSHED*** over, and in no time, the head policemouse met us at the gate.

"We located the third **Doomsday Desolarizer**," he informed us. "It's at the top of the **ROLLER COASTER**. But we have a problem. It's guarded by **robot spiders**!"

"R-robot s-spiders?" I stuttered. "That's a problem with a lot of l-legs."

"Right-o, partner!" Swiftpaws said eagerly. "So we'd better get a *leg up* on the situation."

"**Whaaat?**" I squeaked.

Swiftpaws lifted me up with a **heave** and **plunked** me down in one of the roller-coaster cars. Then he **POPPED** into the seat next to me.

We started moving immediately—and I was **TERRIFIED**! An army of **robot spiders** was marching toward us.

"Swiftpaws, we have to go faster!"

"**IMPOSSIBLE**, partner!" he shouted as the coaster climbed up the track steadily. "We're going uphill!"

The spiders got closer, threatening us with their **CLICKING JAWS**.

"*Bubbling hot fondue!*" I wailed. "How are we going to get out of this?!"

As soon as I said those words, my **superpowers** activated, producing a stream of gooey melted hot fondue that poured over the spiders, drowning them in cheese.

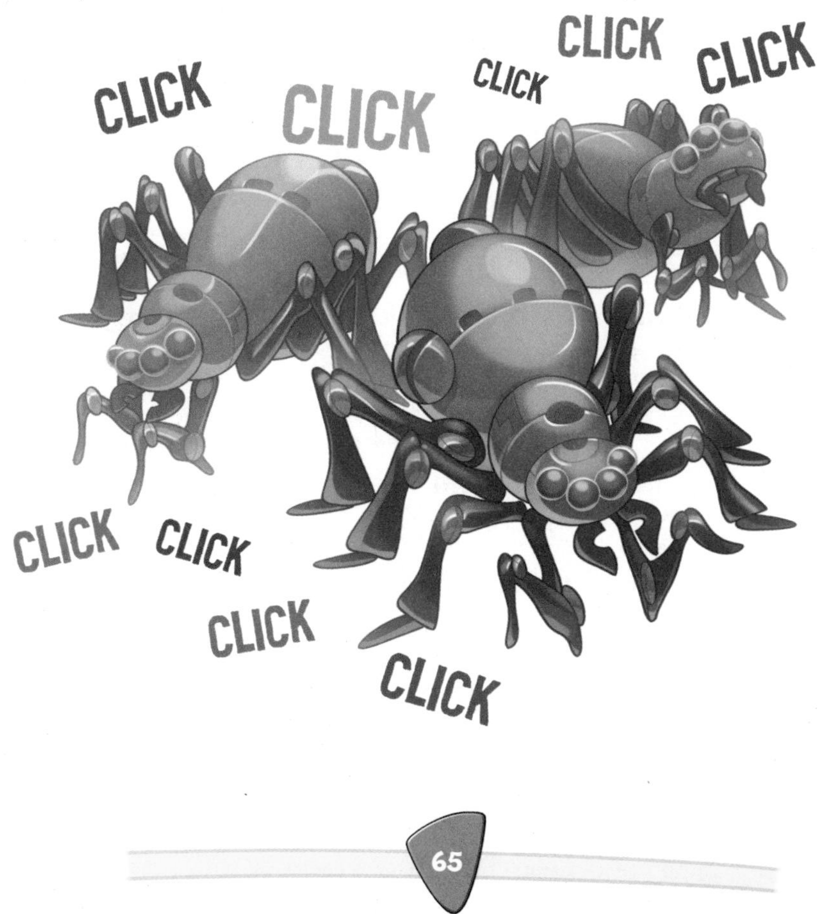

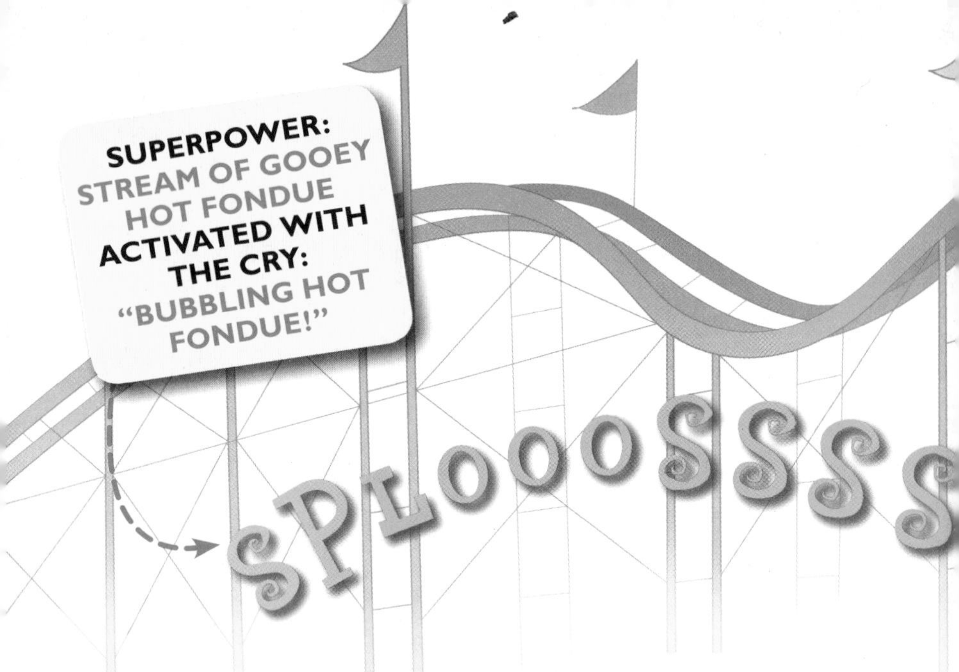

"Bug off, you metal pests!" I rejoiced.

But I had squeaked too soon. A second ARMY of spiders was ahead of us, blocking our way.

Oh no! We were done for!

That is, until Lady Wonderwhiskers's perfectly timed arrival.

"**Scram**, you pieces of junk!" she ordered, holding a metal cable in her paws.

The spiders started to charge, but the

Heromouse was already in flight. With a few **LEAPS**, she tied the cable around the spiders' legs. Then she gave a strong yank, crunching the spiders together. Finally, she swung the tangled mess over the edge of the roller coaster.

Unfortunately, she didn't let go of

the cable in time, and she was pulled right over the edge with them! Without thinking, I dove over and grabbed her in my paws. But now we were in FREE FALL!

"Quick, Superstilton!" she cried. "Activate your landing powers!"

"Salty Parmesan shavings!" I shouted. What landing powers? I didn't know what to do!

Smoosh!

But my supersuit did. Just as we were about to hit the hard ground, a pile of PARMESAN shavings softened our fall.

Whew! Saved by a whisker!

I can't look!
Wheee!
SUPERPOWER:
SOFT PILE OF
CHEESE SHAVINGS
ACTIVATED WITH
THE CRY:
"SALTY PARMESAN
SHAVINGS!"

Trouble in Swiss Square

"Superstilton!" Lady Wonderwhiskers beamed. "You **SAVED** my snout!"

Ahhh . . . my heart melted like warm baked Brie. But the feeling didn't last long. In the next moment, Swiftpaws whizzed by and fell into the cheese shavings between my favorite Heromouse and me.

"While you were *falling* for Wonderwhiskers, I deactivated the third Doomsday Desolarizer!" my partner explained.

I was about to ask how when Proton, Electron, and a heroic-looking **STRANGER** appeared.

"**Monterey Jack!**" my partner said as he turned to face the unfamiliar mouse. "Who are you?"

"You can call me **Super E**!" she declared.

"Who?" I squeaked.

Lady Wonderwhiskers laughed. "Don't you recognize her? It's ELENA!"

"What?" Swiftpaws said, looking stunned. "Oh! Of course. I knew that."

"Let's cut to the chase, Heromice!" Electron said, calling us to ATTENTION. "We absolutely must destroy the fourth Desolarizer before it's too late!"

Beep, beep, beep, beep!

I glanced at my wrist and saw that Tess Technopaws was calling me on my Heromouse watch.

"MACARONI AND CHEESE!" she cried. "We've got trouble! The Sewer Rats'

Sludgemobile just showed up here in Swiss Square."

"*Holey cheese!*" I squealed.

"Can you tell us more, Tess?" Lady Wonderwhiskers prompted.

"It looks like **Tony Sludge** wants to steal the golden statues," she replied. "And he won't let anything or any mouse get in his way . . ."

"I guess Daddy wants to officially be the MOST EVIL VILLAIN," Elena remarked sarcastically.

"**RATFORD** is already here, but he can't hold back the Sewer Rats much longer," Tess went on. "We need you, Heromice!"

"It's almost **noon**," Swiftpaws noted. "What should we do?"

"We could split up again," Electron suggested. "Superstilton, Swiftpaws,

Proton: You three stop Sludge! Lady Wonderwhiskers, Elena, and I will take care of the last Desolarizer. Heromice: We can do it!"

Heromouse vs. "Heromouse"

It was fifteen minutes before noon when Lady Wonderwhiskers, Electron, and Elena reached the outskirts of town. Electron led the way through the DARK, empty streets.

"Look! There!" she called, pointing to a thin black beam rising from the roof of an abandoned warehouse.

"We found it!" Elena said excitedly. "That has to be the fourth Desolarizer. Now we just have to get there and turn it off!" She brushed past Electron and started off in the direction of the warehouse.

"Watch out!" Electron warned. "We don't

want to get **attacked** again."

Elena rolled her eyes. "And what if we do?" she replied. "A real Heromouse is afraid of nothing!"

"Hold on a second," Electron snapped. "You're NOT a real Heromouse. You're a Sludge!"

"And you're just jealous because I'm wearing a supersuit and you're not!" came Elena's retort.

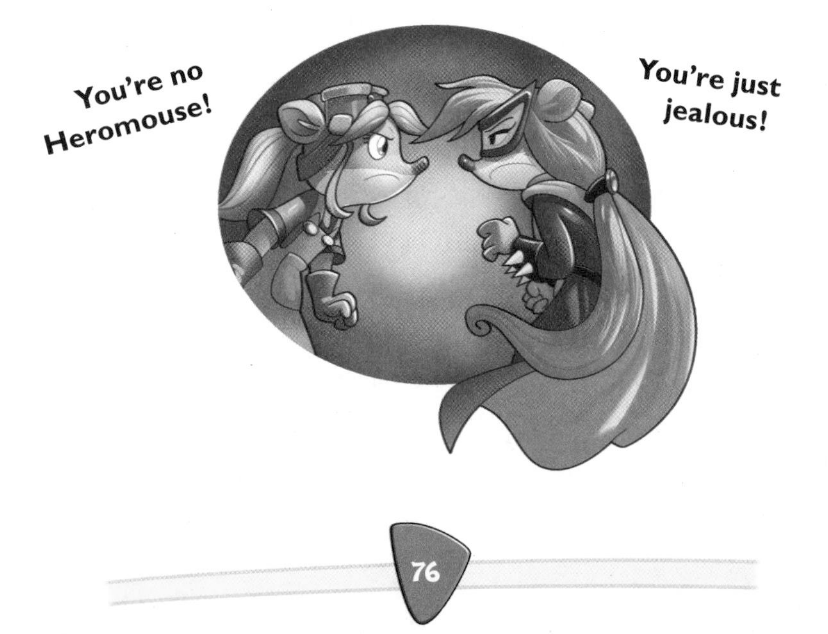

"That's enough, you two!" Lady Wonderwhiskers broke in. "Instead of fighting with one another, we need to save the day—literally! Muskrat City can't stay dark forever!"

The three mice tiptoed into the empty warehouse. It was a maze of endless hallways filled with old boxes and equipment.

"How are we ever going to find this machine?" Elena grumbled.

Suddenly, she heard a sound.

CLICK CLICK CLICK CLICK CLICK

Lady Wonderwhiskers winced. "That's the sound of the robot spiders!"

The mice spun around to see the spiders climbing on top of one another and transforming into a MEGA-ROBOT SPIDER!

Lady Wonderwhiskers was instantly on the move. "Over here, Big creepy! Try to catch me!"

The MEGA-ROBOT lunged forward, but the Heromouse bounded away.

"Electron! Elena! Try to deactivate the Desolarizer while I distract this giant creep!" she shouted.

The two mouselets snapped to attention.

"You can count on us!" Electron cried.

Elena watched the robot carefully. "Electron!" she shouted. "On the highest SPIDER—see that little window?"

"Yes!" Electron replied. "The CONTROLS must be in there!"

"This is a job for Super E!" Elena called back as she grabbed on to the back legs of the mega-robot and hoisted herself up. Then she turned and extended her paw to Electron. "Come on!"

Electron looked at her hesitantly.

"Remember, I'm not a TECHNO NERD like you," the young Sludge said. "I have no idea how to turn that thing off!"

Electron wasn't sure she should trust Elena, but she had a point. They had to turn off the mega-robot and save

Come on!
Um . . .

Come and get me!

Lady Wonderwhiskers! Electron made up her mind and grabbed Elena's paw. Next, the two mice managed to scramble into the robot spider's CONTROL ROOM while it continued chasing Lady Wonderwhiskers.

"Okay, do I cut the RED wire or the blue one?" Electron mumbled to herself as she examined the controls, scratching her snout nervously. "Or maybe I tie the green one to the yellow one. Or do I press this PURPLE button?"

"Come on, nerd," Elena urged encouragingly. "You can do it!"

Electron took a deep breath and leaned over the controls. Finally, she cut the RED wire, turned a screw counterclockwise, then pressed a green button three times. The mega-robot screeched and raised its front legs, making the mice tumble off.

Then, suddenly, they heard a low whirring sound and the spider powered down to a complete stop.

"EXCELLENT WORK, mouselets!" cheered Lady Wonderwhiskers. "I knew you could do it!" she said with a wink.

"Well, Elena . . . I mean, **Super E** . . ." Electron began. "I have to admit: You're as **brave** as any Heromouse!"

Elena's eyes grew wide with surprise at the compliment, but she quickly recovered.

"Whatever," she said. "Of course I'm brave. And uh . . . you're pretty brave yourself, for a NERD."

Electron grinned. "Let's go. We have a Desolarizer to find. Time's running out: The Dome of Doom becomes permanent in five minutes!"

Best Leading Rat

While Lady Wonderwhiskers and the mouselets **explored** the warehouse, Proton and I rushed over to **Swiss Square**.

"Oh, **sour cream and crackers**!" Tess exclaimed when we arrived. "Tony's stealing all the **GOLDEN STATUES**, and his henchmice are guarding the stage. We can't get near it!"

Proton surveyed the stage area. "Sludge's Sewer Rats are using **BE BLIND BLASTERS** to **attack** Ratford's policemice!"

He was right. One, Two, Three, and Slickfur had even **cornered** Commissioner Ratford himself behind a police car.

But Ratford wasn't giving up. "Heromice!"

he shouted. "You have to stop Tony Sludge!"

But where was Tony?

A second later, I had my answer. Tony had climbed the stage and was admiring the **Golden Sun Awards**, a sneer on

his snout. He picked up a statue.

"The award for **Most Evil Crime Rat** in Muskrat City goes to . . . Tony Sludge!" He cackled evilly.

He dropped the award into a big sack and grabbed another. "And the award for **Most Handsome Rat** in Muskrat City goes to . . . Tony Sludge!" Then he dropped that in his bag, too.

"And the award for Smelliest Sewer Rat goes to—" Swiftpaws called out, interrupting him, "Tony Sludge!"

Tony glared offstage.

"What are you doing here, SUPERFOOL?!" he asked, scowling.

"Your Doomsday Desolarizers have all been deactivated!" I burst out.

The leader of the Sewer Rats shot a look at his henchmice. "You DIMWITTED fools! Get those meddlesome Heromice!"

One, Two, and Three went into attack mode. But Swiftpaws was ready. "Supersuit: Bowling-Ball Mode!" he cried.

My partner rolled into the bodyguards and . . . STRIKE! All three went down!

"Ha! No fool was SPARED!" Swiftpaws celebrated.

But right then, Slickfur hit him with the BE BLIND BLASTER.

"Super Swiss slices! Everything is BLACK!" moaned Swiftpaws, clutching his eyes.

"Great cubes of cheddar!" I shouted. "Leave my friend alone!"

Slickfur did: He aimed his blaster at me instead. **AAHHH!** I shielded my eyes and braced for the worst. But that's when a **wall** of cheddar cubes **MAGICALLY** appeared, blocking his shot.

Yikes! That had been a close call. But then I heard Ratford cry out, "Watch your back, Superstilton!"

Ack! All of a sudden, I felt myself being lifted into the air. Tony Sludge had snuck up from behind and picked me up with his bare paws!

"It's one minute until noon, when the dome freezes forever," he jeered. "I've taken your SUN and"—he pointed to his heavy sack of statues—"your GOLDEN SUNS. Ha, ha, ha!"

CRACK, CRACK.

Were those my bones cracking in Tony's paws?

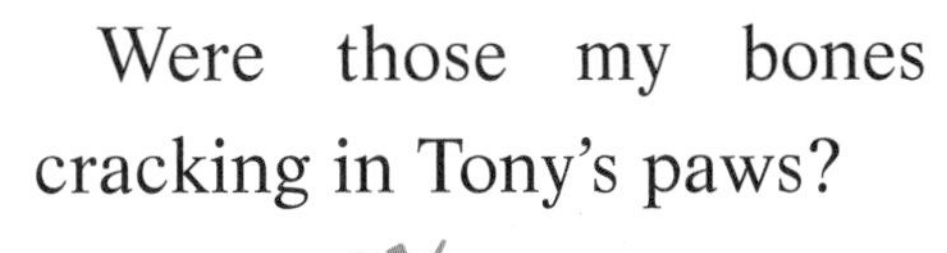

The sound grew louder and I was starting to see

Now it's just the two of us . . .

SUPERPOWER: WALL OF CHEDDAR ACTIVATED WITH THE CRY: "GREAT CUBES OF CHEDDAR!"

PATCHES OF LIGHT above me. What was happening? Cheese on a stick, surely this was THE END!

But wait. Tony heard the sounds, too. We both looked up and saw cracks crawling across the black dome above us. The light was SUNLIGHT coming through the cracks!

"W-what?" Tony stammered. "Wait. How?"

"CREAM CHEESE AND JELLY!" Swiftpaws squeaked. "The dome is breaking! Lady Wonderwhiskers, Super E, and Electron did it! They deactivated the last Desolarizers!"

It's the sun!
W-what?
Wait. How?

SUNNY DAYS

In less than a minute, the noon sun was drenching Muskrat City with warm, bright light. We had gotten so used to the DARKNESS that for a few seconds, none of us could see a thing—including TONY.

"Aahh! I can't see!" he said. Then he let go of me to paw at his eyes. I dropped to the ground and **raced** away, quiet as a mouse.

Slickfur recovered next and sprinted to the Sludgemobile to make his escape. "ONE, TWO, THREE!" he hissed. "Let's go!" The henchmice didn't wait to be told twice. They climbed into the car and Slickfur revved the engine.

"Boss!" Slickfur squeaked to Sludge. "Come on!"

By now, Tony's eyes had adjusted. "You scaredy-rats!" he roared. "I didn't order a retreat! No one beats Tony Sludge—"

The leader of the Sewer Rats was so riled up that he didn't see *Commissioner Ratford* behind him.

"Tony Sludge, you're under arrest!"

Sludge's tail dropped and he took a step back.

"Well, uh . . . maybe a **strategic retreat** isn't such a bad idea."

And with that, he *ran* toward the Sludgemobile.

Nooo! The Sewer Rat was **getting away**—again!

"**MOLDY SMOKED MOZZARELLA BALLS!**" I protested. "We have to get him!"

My **Supersuit** triggered my powers. In a flash, a **downpour** of huge mozzarella balls rained on Swiss Square.

The mozzarella balls dropped one after another on the Sludgemobile and Tony's

henchmice. When one hit Tony right on the snout, Swiftpaws and I went to POUNCE. But the Sewer Rat grabbed the ball and launched it at us instead.

"You won today," he snarled. "But this is nothing! Next time, Muskrat City will truly be DOOMED!"

And, before we knew it, the Sludgemobile had disappeared underground with Tony Sludge inside.

The Sewer Rats had gotten away, but it felt like a new day in Swiss Square. Soon it was filled with mice coming outside to soak in the SUN.

"Superstilton, Swiftpaws!" The sound of Lady Wonderwhiskers, Electron, and Elena calling to us was music to my ears.

"You did it!" they squeaked happily.

"Well," Swiftpaws replied, "you did it

yourselves! You ***destroyed*** the **DOME** just in time!"

Lady Wonderwhiskers grinned. "Thanks to Electron and—"

"Me!" Elena boasted. "You would never have deactivated the **Desolarizers** without **Super E**, right?"

The young Sludge ignored Electron's eye roll.

"Well, I'd better head home before Daddy finds out," Elena said. "And I didn't even get to meet Rob Squeak! I wasted all my time getting you NERDS out of trouble."

"Nobody asked for your help!" Electron replied, annoyed. "You *insisted* on coming along!"

"Please don't fight!" Proton broke in. "We're grateful for your help, Elena. You lent us a paw, and . . ." Proton glanced off into the distance. "Hold on! I'll be right back!" Then he disappeared into the crowd.

A few minutes later, he returned with another mouse: the TV STAR Rob Squeak!

Elena's eyes grew **wide** as her snout turned **Beet ReD**.

"Rob Squeak, this is Super E," Proton said.

"She helped save **MUSKRAT CITY**. She's a big fan of yours and . . . a **HEROMOUSE**. Would you give her an *autograph*?"

"But of course!" Mr. Squeak said, whiskers gleaming. "Tell me, what should I write?"

Elena paused, then lit up with an idea. "Write: 'to Super E, the bravest new Heromouse'!"

"Sure," the star replied as he scrawled his autograph. "Thank you for everything, Heromouse!"

Then he shook Elena's paw, combed his other paw through his fur, and strutted away.

Elena was so overjoyed that she turned to Proton and KISSED him right on his snout. "Thank you, thank you, thank you, Proton! You're the BEST!"

Finally, she turned to Electron.

"See ya, nerd," she squeaked, sticking out her tongue before she took off.

Electron groaned. "Can you believe her, Proton?!" she asked, rolling her eyes. "Proton?"

But the young mouselet was frozen with

a GOOFY expression on his snout. “Oh, for cheese’s sake, you’re blushing like a pizza with TRIPLE TOMATO SAUCE on top!” Electron cried.

All Proton could do was turn even redder.

Total Eclipse of the Fur

Slowly, **MUSKRAT CITY** returned to normal. Swiss Square filled with mice basking in the sun after the *longest night* of their lives.

With the Sun back (and the recovery of the bag of **Golden Sun** statues that Tony had dropped), Mayor Powerpaws was finally able to proceed with the awards ceremony.

"I don't know about you, partner," Swiftpaws told me. "But after all this hard work, I'm craving something **scrumptious**."

RUUUMMMBLE . . .

Golden Sun Awards
Congratulations!
Thank you!
Hooray!

My stomach agreed. I hadn't eaten in hours!

"Superstilton, why don't you stop by Heromice Headquarters before going home?" Tess suggested. "I could bake you your favorite cheese croissants!"

"That sounds great!" I exclaimed. "Tess, you're my favorite chef and scientist!"

"And not just because you're the only chef and scientist," Lady Wonderwhiskers said, making us all chuckle.

After a delicious snack of WARM CROISSANTS with perfectly melted mozzarella, I waved good-bye to my friends and flew off for New Mouse City. I couldn't wait to curl up and take a nap! Looking back at the longest night ever, I realized I had gotten no sleep!

When I landed in New Mouse City, the sun

was high in the sky and masses of rodents were out and about. I noticed that everyone was wearing strange SUNGLASSES, hats, and visors. Did I land in the middle of a SUMMER CHEESE DAY PARADE?

Before I could figure out what was going on, something caught my eye. I looked down

and my fur immediately stood on end. I had forgotten that when I left for Muskrat City, I had been on assignment at Monsieur le Rat's spa, and I had been wearing only a bathrobe. Now that my supersuit was gone, that's all I was wearing right now! BURNT BRIE ON A STICK! How embarrassing!

My face turned redder than a grilled red pepper as my eyes darted around me. But

strangely enough, no one even noticed my predicament! The mice around me were all staring up at the **sky**. I shot a look upward just as the sky was turning **BLACK**. It was almost as if the sun—**OH NOOO**! Not again!

Stinky slices of Swiss! Had Tony and the Sewer Rats activated a **DOME OF DOOM** over New Mouse City, too?!

"Ooooooh!" the mice around me exclaimed. Huh? Instead of crying out in **horror**, the mice in the crowd were holding up their special **SUNGLASSES** and gasping in awe.

Hmmm . . . those glasses looked familiar. Where had I seen them before? Aha! It came to me in a flash. I remembered that a rare **SOLAR ECLIPSE** had been forecast for Mouse Island that afternoon. I had

Oh no!
Amazing!
Wow!
Incredible!

written an article for *The Rodent's Gazette* explaining the natural phenomenon, which happens when the MOON lines up between the EARTH and the sun. It was the moon that was momentarily blocking the sun—not another Dome of Doom! Thank goodmouse!

Luckily for me, everyone was so captivated by the ECLIPSE that they didn't see me in my robe! Whew! Humiliation avoided by the tips of my **whiskers**!

I *clutched* my robe tightly and scurried home in the dark as fast as my paws could carry me.

As I wove my way through the packed streets, I realized that, unlike in Muskrat City, this sudden blackout was a total stroke of GOOD LUCK!

This Heromouse wins again!

I need to get home!

DON'T MISS ANY HEROMICE BOOKS!

#1 Mice to the Rescue!

#2 Robot Attack

#3 Flood Mission

#4 The Perilous Plants

#5 The Invisible Thief

#6 Dinosaur Danger

#7 Time Machine Trouble

#8 Charge of the Clones

#9 Insect Invasion

#10 Sweet Dreams, Sewer Rats!

#11 Revenge of the Mini-Mice

Be sure to read all my fabumouse adventures!
#1 Lost Treasure of the Emerald Eye
#2 The Curse of the Cheese Pyramid
#3 Cat and Mouse in a Haunted House
#4 I'm Too Fond of My Fur!
#5 Four Mice Deep in the Jungle
#6 Paws Off, Cheddarface!
#7 Red Pizzas for a Blue Count
#8 Attack of the Bandit Cats
#9 A Fabumouse Vacation for Geronimo
#10 All Because of a Cup of Coffee
#11 It's Halloween, You 'Fraidy Mouse!
#12 Merry Christmas, Geronimo!
#13 The Phantom of the Subway
#14 The Temple of the Ruby of Fire
#15 The Mona Mousa Code
#16 A Cheese-Colored Camper
#17 Watch Your Whiskers, Stilton!
#18 Shipwreck on the Pirate Islands
#19 My Name Is Stilton, Geronimo Stilton
#20 Surf's Up, Geronimo!
#21 The Wild, Wild West
#22 The Secret of Cacklefur Castle
A Christmas Tale

#23 Valentine's Day Disaster

#24 Field Trip to Niagara Falls

#25 The Search for Sunken Treasure

#26 The Mummy with No Name

#27 The Christmas Toy Factory

#28 Wedding Crasher

#29 Down and Out Down Under

#30 The Mouse Island Marathon

#31 The Mysterious Cheese Thief

Christmas Catastrophe

#32 Valley of the Giant Skeletons

#33 Geronimo and the Gold Medal Mystery

#34 Geronimo Stilton, Secret Agent

#35 A Very Merry Christmas

#36 Geronimo's Valentine

#37 The Race Across America

#38 A Fabumouse School Adventure

#39 Singing Sensation

#40 The Karate Mouse

#41 Mighty Mount Kilimanjaro

#42 The Peculiar Pumpkin Thief

#43 I'm Not a Supermouse!

#44 The Giant Diamond Robbery

#45 Save the White Whale!

#46 The Haunted Castle

#47 Run for the Hills, Geronimo!

#48 The Mystery in Venice

#49 The Way of the Samurai

#50 This Hotel Is Haunted!

#51 The Enormouse Pearl Heist

#52 Mouse in Space!

#53 Rumble in the Jungle

#54 Get into Gear, Stilton!

#55 The Golden Statue Plot

#56 Flight of the Red Bandit

The Hunt for the Golden Book

#57 The Stinky Cheese Vacation

#58 The Super Chef Contest

#59 Welcome to Moldy Manor

The Hunt for the Curious Cheese

#60 The Treasure of Easter Island

#61 Mouse House Hunter

#62 Mouse Overboard!

The Hunt for the Secret Papyrus

#63 The Cheese Experiment

#64 Magical Mission

#65 Bollywood Burglary

The Hunt for the Hundredth Key

#66 Operation: Secret Recipe

#67 The Chocolate Chase

Don't miss any of my adventures in the Kingdom of Fantasy!

THE KINGDOM OF FANTASY

THE QUEST FOR PARADISE:
THE RETURN TO THE KINGDOM OF FANTASY

THE AMAZING VOYAGE:
THE THIRD ADVENTURE IN THE KINGDOM OF FANTASY

THE DRAGON PROPHECY:
THE FOURTH ADVENTURE IN THE KINGDOM OF FANTASY

THE VOLCANO OF FIRE:
THE FIFTH ADVENTURE IN THE KINGDOM OF FANTASY

THE SEARCH FOR TREASURE:
THE SIXTH ADVENTURE IN THE KINGDOM OF FANTASY

THE ENCHANTED CHARMS:
THE SEVENTH ADVENTURE IN THE KINGDOM OF FANTASY

THE PHOENIX OF DESTINY:
AN EPIC KINGDOM OF FANTASY ADVENTURE

THE HOUR OF MAGIC:
THE EIGHTH ADVENTURE IN THE KINGDOM OF FANTASY

THE WIZARD'S WAND:
THE NINTH ADVENTURE IN THE KINGDOM OF FANTASY

THE SHIP OF SECRETS:
THE TENTH ADVENTURE IN THE KINGDOM OF FANTASY

THE DRAGON OF FORTUNE:
AN EPIC KINGDOM OF FANTASY ADVENTURE

Don't miss any of these exciting Thea Sisters adventures!

Thea Stilton and the Dragon's Code

Thea Stilton and the Mountain of Fire

Thea Stilton and the Ghost of the Shipwreck

Thea Stilton and the Secret City

Thea Stilton and the Mystery in Paris

Thea Stilton and the Cherry Blossom Adventure

Thea Stilton and the Star Castaways

Thea Stilton: Big Trouble in the Big Apple

Thea Stilton and the Ice Treasure

Thea Stilton and the Secret of the Old Castle

Thea Stilton and the Blue Scarab Hunt

Thea Stilton and the Prince's Emerald

Thea Stilton and the Mystery on the Orient Express

Thea Stilton and the Dancing Shadows

Thea Stilton and the Legend of the Fire Flowers

Thea Stilton and the Spanish Dance Mission

Thea Stilton and the Journey to the Lion's Den

Thea Stilton and the Great Tulip Heist

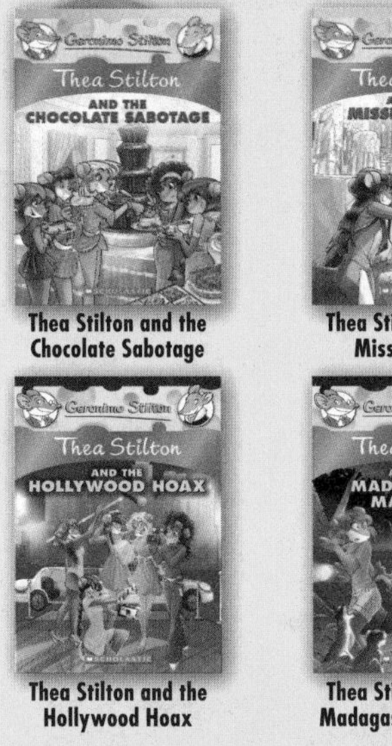

Thea Stilton and the Chocolate Sabotage

Thea Stilton and the Missing Myth

Thea Stilton and the Lost Letters

Thea Stilton and the Tropical Treasure

Thea Stilton and the Hollywood Hoax

Thea Stilton and the Madagascar Madness

Thea Stilton and the Frozen Fiasco

Thea Stilton and the Venice Masquerade

And check out my fabumouse special editions!

THEA STILTON: THE JOURNEY TO ATLANTIS

THEA STILTON: THE SECRET OF THE FAIRIES

THEA STILTON: THE SECRET OF THE SNOW

THEA STILTON: THE CLOUD CASTLE

THEA STILTON: THE TREASURE OF THE SEA

THEA STILTON: THE LAND OF FLOWERS

MEET GERONIMO STILTONIX

He is a spacemouse — the Geronimo Stilton of a parallel universe! He is captain of the spaceship *MouseStar 1*. While flying through the cosmos, he visits distant planets and meets crazy aliens. His adventures are out of this world!

#1 Alien Escape

#2 You're Mine, Captain!

#3 Ice Planet Adventure

#4 The Galactic Goal

#5 Rescue Rebellion

#6 The Underwater Planet

#7 Beware! Space Junk!

#8 Away in a Star Sled

#9 Slurp Monster Showdown

#10 Pirate Spacecat Attack

#11 We'll Bite Your Tail, Geronimo!

Meet GERONIMO STILTONOOT

He is a cavemouse — Geronimo Stilton's ancient ancestor! He runs the stone newspaper in the prehistoric village of Old Mouse City. From dealing with dinosaurs to dodging meteorites, his life in the Stone Age is full of adventure!

#1 The Stone of Fire

#2 Watch Your Tail!

#3 Help, I'm in Hot Lava!

#4 The Fast and the Frozen

#5 The Great Mouse Race

#6 Don't Wake the Dinosaur!

#7 I'm a Scaredy-Mouse!

#8 Surfing for Secrets

#9 Get the Scoop, Geronimo!

#10 My Autosaurus Will Win!

#11 Sea Monster Surprise

#12 Paws Off the Pearl!

#13 The Smelly Search

#14 Shoo, Caveflies!

#15 A Mammoth Mystery

DEAR MOUSE FRIENDS,
THANKS FOR READING, AND
FAREWELL TILL THE NEXT BOOK.
IT'LL BE ANOTHER
WHISKER-LICKING-GOOD
ADVENTURE, AND THAT'S
A PROMISE!